THE GINGERBREAD BOY

story retold by Jim Lawrence • illustrated by Tim Hildebrandt

Modern Publishing
A Division of Unisystems, Inc.
New York, New York 10022

Once upon a time, a little old lady and a little old man lived all by themselves in a little old house.

"Wouldn't it be lovely if we had a special treat today?" asked the little old lady. "I think I will make us a gingerbread boy!"

"Ah, yes! Do, my dear!" said the little old man. "Nothing can beat your gingerbread!"

So the little old lady made a beautiful gingerbread boy with raisin eyes and a cherry nose and a licorice candy mouth. His coat buttons were marshmallows.

"What a handsome young chap!" said the little old man.

Then his good wife put the pan in the oven and closed the door.

Soon a delicious smell of baked gingerbread filled the kitchen.

"I'm sure he must be ready now!" said the little old lady.

She opened the oven door, and out popped the Gingerbread Boy!

"Oh my stars! There he goes!" cried the little old lady.

And out the door and down the front walk ran the Gingerbread Boy.

Before anyone could stop him, he jumped over the gate and scooted off down the road!

"Stop! Stop!" shouted the little old man.

"Come back, come back!" cried the little old lady, and they both ran after him.

But the funny little boy was having the time of his life. Instead of coming back, he laughed and shouted:

> *"I'll run, run, run!*
> *And jump for joy!*
> *You can't catch me,*
> *I'm the Gingerbread Boy!"*

On and on ran the Gingerbread Boy on his funny little
gingerbread legs.

"Moo moo!" said a cow in the meadow. "What smells so good?"
When she saw the runaway, she forgot all about chewing her cud.

"Stop, stop, little Gingerbread Boy!" she mooed. "I think you would
taste much better than grass!"

But the little chap just laughed and called out:

"I've run away from a little old lady
and a little old man!
And I can run away from cows,
I can, I can!"

So the cow left her shady spot under the trees and took off after
him—*ker-bump, ker-bobble! ker-flobbity-flobble!*
But she couldn't catch him.

A horse was grazing in the field. It raised its head and sniffed the breeze.

"Um-m-m-m, what smells so good?" neighed the horse. Then he saw the yummy-looking little fellow dashing down the road.

"Stop, stop, little Gingerbread Boy!" the horse whinnied. "Something tells me you would make delicious fodder!"

But the Gingerbread Boy just chuckled and shouted back:

"*I've run away from a cow and a lady*
and a little old man!
And I can run away from you,
I can, I can!"

Gallop-a-gallop-a-gallop! came the horse. But the Gingerbread Boy was right. The horse couldn't catch him, either!

Some farmers stopped hoeing and mowing and threshing when they saw the strange little runaway go by.

How good he smelled! Their mouths began to water!

"Stop, stop, little Gingerbread Boy!" they shouted. "It's lunchtime! Wouldn't you like to stay for lunch?"

"No, indeed," laughed the Gingerbread Boy. "Not if I'm going to be the lunch!"

"I'm going to run, run, run
and jump for joy!
You can't catch me,
I'm the Gingerbread Boy!"

Faster and faster ran the
Gingerbread Boy! The little lad was so crisp
and light, he could go like the wind!

What fun it was to out race everyone!
Just thinking about it made him hop and skip and jump for joy!

Suddenly he saw a fox peeking out at him from the woods.

"Ho, ho, ho!" whooped the Gingerbread Boy.
"No use sniffing the air like that, Mr. Fox!"

"I've run away from some farmers and
a horse and a cow and a little
old lady and a little old man!
And I can run away from you too,
I can, I can!"

"Of course you can, my boy!" said the sly old fox.
"I wouldn't dream of trying to catch someone as fast
as you!"

But finally the Gingerbread Boy came to a river. What to do now? There was no time to lose! He knew that if he jumped in the water and tried to swim, he would get all soggy and mushy. Before he got to the other side, he might even go all to pieces!

Suddenly the fox appeared. "No problem, my dear boy," said the fox. "Jump on my tail and I will carry you across the river!"

"Ah, just the thing!" said the Gingerbread Boy, who didn't see any reason not to go with the fox.

Once they were out in the river, the sly old fox said, "Oops! You may get wet perched out there on my tail. Better hop up on my back, young fellow!"

So the Gingerbread Boy did.

Soon the water got deeper, and the Gingerbread Boy was afraid his toes might get wet.

"Tell you what, my boy," said the fox. "Jump up on my nose. That will keep you high and dry till we reach the other side."

"Good idea!" said the cookie kid. So he did.

The sly old fox chuckled deep inside. "How yummy this gingerbread is going to taste!" he thought.

Then he threw back his head and tossed the Gingerbread Boy in the air, expecting to snap him up in one bite!